this
little 🌳 ORCHARD
book belongs to

....

....

For Angus T.P.

ORCHARD BOOKS
96 Leonard Street, London EC2A 4XD
Orchard Books Australia
32/45-51 Huntley Street, Alexandria NSW 2015
1 84362 225 4
First published in Great Britain in 2000
This edition published in 2003
Illustrations © Penny Dann 2000
The right of Penny Dann to be identified as
the illustrator of this work has been asserted by her
in accordance with the Copyright, Designs and Patents Act, 1988.
A CIP catalogue record for this book is available from the British Library.
Printed in Italy

Teddy Bear, Teddy Bear, turn around

Penny Dann

little ORCHARD

Teddy bear, teddy bear turn around.

Teddy bear, teddy bear
touch the ground.

Teddy bear, teddy bear touch your nose.

Teddy bear, teddy bear
touch your toes.

Teddy bear, teddy bear go upstairs.

Teddy bear, teddy bear say your prayers.

Teddy bear, teddy bear
turn out the light.

Teddy bear, teddy bear say, "Goodnight!"